Dependable
Dora
Dove

by Christine Harder Tangvald
illustrated by Rusty Fletcher

Text © 1998 by Christine Harder Tangvald
Illustrations © 1998 The Standard Publishing Company, Cincinnati, Ohio
A division of Standex International Corporation. All rights reserved
Printed in the United States of America
Designed by Coleen Davis. ISBN 0-7847-0835-5

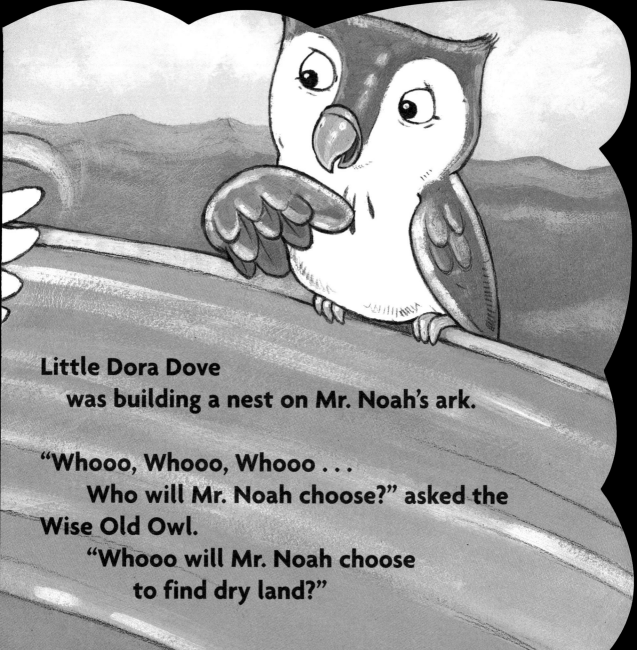

Little Dora Dove
    was building a nest on Mr. Noah's ark.

"Whooo, Whooo, Whooo . . .
    Who will Mr. Noah choose?" asked the
Wise Old Owl.
    "Whooo will Mr. Noah choose
        to find dry land?"

"Mr. Noah will choose me, of course!"
said Regal the Eagle,
"because I am *regal*,
    and I am an eagle.
Oh, yes, Mr. Noah
    will choose me."

Little Dora Dove
    kept building
    her nest.

Swoosh,   Swish,   SWOOSH!
went Dartin' B. Martin.

"Mr. Noah needs a *fast* bird to find
dry land," said Dartin' B. Martin.
"He will choose a fast bird . . .
like me!"

Swoosh, Swish,
SWOOSH!

Little Dora Dove
kept building her nest.

"Twitter, twitter, twitter, twitter.
Chirp! Chirp! CHIRP!"
said Sherri Canary.
"I think Mr. Noah will choose
a bird that can *sing* . . .
a bird like me!
Twitter, twitter, twitter, twitter.
Chirp! Chirp! CHIRP!"

Little Dora Dove kept
building her nest.

"Ahem,"
said Mrs. Buzzard.
"Maybe Mr. Noah needs a *handsome* bird . . .
a bird with some class and dignity . . .
and extreme *good* looks . . .
a bird like *my* husband!"

Little Dora Dove
kept building her nest.

"Oh, PUL-EEEZE!"
     said Missy Prissy Parrot.
"I am the *good-looking* one here!
     Just look at my gorgeous red and
yellow and blue and green feathers!
     Surely, Mr. Noah will choose me!"

Missy Prissy Parrot PUFFED and FLUFFED.

Little Dora Dove
     kept building her nest.

"AWK,   SQUAWK!"
screeched Hank Hawk.
"You birds don't have a chance!"

"To find dry land,
Mr. Noah will send a bird
that can GLIDE and SWOOP,
DIVE and LOOP!
And that bird is *me!*"

Little Dora Dove
kept building her nest.

"Because she is *humble*,"
said Mr. Noah.
    "Because she is *dependable*,"
    said Mr. Noah.
"I choose Dora Dove!
    Oh, yes, I choose
Dependable Dora Dove to
    go and find dry land."

"Gulp!" went all
the birds together.
    "Gulp, Gulp,   GASP!"

Little Dora flew off
   to find the dry land.

"God go with you, Dora Dove!"
   said Mr. Noah.
   All the other birds waited.
   They waited . . . and waited . . .

   They waited . . . and waited . . .
        and waited.

Then . . .
    there was a speck
        in the sky.

Then . . .
    there was a spot
        in the sky.

Then . . .
    there was *Dependable* Dora Dove
    with a branch in her beak!

"YAY-hooRAY!"
        cried Mr. Noah.
"YAY-hooRAY!"
        cried all the birds together.
        "She did it!
        Dependable Dora Dove
                found *dry land* for
                all of us!"

"I knew you could do it, Dora Dove," said Mr. Noah. "I just knew it!"

Then *Dependable* Little Dora Dove quietly finished building her nest.